Love Vignettes

SONNETS

Donald W. Murphy

1997
LaRena Press
El Dorado Hills, California

Revised Edition ©1997 Donald Wayne Murphy
All rights reserved.
First Edition printed 1982

Book and cover design by Elizabeth Petersen
Rose photograph ©CMCD, Inc.
Printed in the United States of America.

Published by LaRena Press
Post Office Box 5378
El Dorado Hills, California 95762-5378

Library of Congress Catalog Number: 97-70957
ISBN 0-9655599-1-2 (casebound)
ISBN 0-9655599-2-0 (trade paper)

For my father, James Woodrow Murphy
whose Love has sustained me for 46 years.

Acknowledgments

Many acknowledgments in books are gratuitous at best. No one, not even an artist, completes a work without considerable help from others. This book would never have been completed without the assistance of my wife.

I would also like to thank those who offered suggestions and constructive criticism on the book design, especially Laura Wagner.

Preface

When I was sixteen years old and a senior in high school, I took English composition. For my senior project I decided to do a paper on the nature of human love. I read Emerson's essay on the subject and many other authors. I honestly tried to write that paper. But as the more wise among you may have already guessed, I never finished that paper.

I guess you can say that this book of sonnets, *Love Vignettes,* is a completion, some thirty years later, of that failed attempt. The difference is my experience and struggle with love. *Love Vignettes* are modern sonnets which represent the essence distilled from an honest attempt to work through the problems of romantic and Godly love. This at a time when people find it difficult to communicate honestly, let alone love each other.

These sonnets have been heavily revised from the first edition. If you have a problem with that, just think of it as evolutionary poetry. I am not the first poet to have revised poems between editions.

The revisions, I hope, merely serve to better communicate to you the reader. And after all, poetry is communication.

I chose the sonnet form for this expression of what I have come to understand about love for the same reason many others before me have chosen its "... scanty plot of ground." Because within its confines there is considerable freedom, yet you are forced to say what you mean in not many words.

At the time I first wrote these sonnets I was in rebellion against the men of my generation who tended to bury their weaknesses beneath ego-machoism. They were not willing to explore their deeper feelings about love. They could not even admit that they felt pain and sorrow. I am happy to see that within only fifteen years, the men of my generation have become more willing to express a more balanced nature.

The religious sentiments remain strong in these sonnets and are still the result of this poet's calling. We strain to hear distant music; yearn with our souls to grasp eternal reasons; and seek to harmonize the notes we hear with the melody of our own lives. For me this has led to a deep sense of the spiritual-mystical nature of our existence as reflected in Sonnet 53:

> *We poets often peer with prying eyes*
> *Where lowly man is forbidden to see.*
> *We are contracted as earthly spies*
> *To steal back paradise lost and glory*
> *Forsaken for too much love of our minds.*

Finally, if it had not been for my father who gave me my first book of poetry at age seven, I never would have written these sonnets. He is dead now, but every time I sit with my children and read poetry aloud, I think of him and the wonderful legacy he left his children. Parents, read to your children.

I

O' to be without hope. It is to be
Thrown into some bottomless pit, or set
Adrift upon the angry, restless sea;
Forever locked away. To have met
With Life's woe and never, never to know
That beyond yonder horizon there lies
Light that was, is, always has been to show:
The life that is hopeful never dies
And finding this truth it embarks upon
A journey that will last forever long.
Leaving despair to wither alone
Its soul shall rise singing a brand new song.
> And when at last it would change, it must find
> That life within that points without the mind.

2

To draw you to myself would be contempt,
Though every fiber of my being cries
Out to possess you. Please, make no attempt
To convince my heart, now burdened with lies,
To turn from its conviction. To do so
Cripples my soul, blinds my eye from seeing.
The you that I would possess I now know
Fades in the possession of its being.
Being coveted and not truly loved
You would sense the violation of self.
So let us dwell only on things above;
Let's place our base affections on the shelf.
> Friendship's not to be had by possession,
> But by making an inward concession.

3

Unspoken words hang on my heart like frost
In some gray-bleak winter, chilling my soul.
I could not say that which had a high cost:
The loss of you, and darkness black like coal.
I wait from winter to winter, hoping
The Divine will my speech overpower;
So that instead of this boyish moping
My cold mouth with springtime grace will shower
On you that with which my heart's encumbered,
And fears for the loss of you to speak:
I don't know you well, though you I've numbered
Amongst those who are the most dear to me.
> You are among the most rarest of finds:
> The temptation's great your riches to mine.

4

I look into your eyes and there I find
The love for which my heart has been at bay;
Knowing all the while Fate has been unkind,
Making me wait 'til I myself betray.
I am so wrong to blame impartial Fate.
For it was my own impatience that made
Time a burden to me. I could not wait
For my honest due. So I took a spade
When I should've taken a heart. Too late
In my sparse life I have found you; and though
I belong to another, I feel hate
For my past mistake, and pain and sorrow.
> Don't despise me because I waited not;
> Rather, hold me close and remove this blot.

5

Do not add that injury to us though
Pleasure it would seem to bring: a false love
Or lust. I cannot help but let you go
To seek things which dwell in heaven above.
Don't see me with your eyes but with your soul;
Don't bind me with physical addiction
Until I am your slave in some dark hole.
Who would rescue us from this affliction?
Would you, after your body's wallowed in
Ecstasy, be able to break free and
Wrestle to earth uncompromising sin,
Freeing me and you both from this quicksand?
    Let us not bind one another with lust;
    But let's keep one another in Gods' Trust.

6

Are we not looking for a reason to
Justify our lust, thereby breeding in
Each other disgust; betraying God, who
Has thus joined us to protect us from sin?
The challenge is this: to resist that which
Would tempt us from the love we should cherish;
And instead hold fast to the last thin stitch
Of Truth which guides us so we won't perish.
Do I love you? Mortal conflict within
Me bears witness to my devotion to
You. I strive endlessly your Love to win:
Hoping that our Love will not make us blue.
    But this must be known above all things known:
    For love of you I would myself disown.

7

O' what joy I find in that concession:
Not binding yourself to me. Having not
Had by having, and so by possession
Deceived, you now understand that the lot
Of those who confuse Love with Lust is to
Languish in insensitivity. For,
Love's not Love which depends on feelings. Who
Would suffer such vile deceit, if not for
The lack of Divine perception. Who for
The sake of a moment's bliss would sacrifice
Eternal life. Would you, knowing the score?
What is gained by Divine Love is not a vice.
    For of all things present and all things past,
    Only real Love, not perjured Lust, will last.

8

Of my very self you have robbed me:
Flesh of my flesh held hostage by your fears.
My soul is in torment, this cannot be.
All my heart's sorrow turns to endless tears
Which cascade down, down my quivering cheeks,
Cutting deep furrows where yesterday dwelt
Hopeful youth. Now, it's weeks added to weeks
Since I have seen the life that was mine; knelt
Beside my youngest darling, felt her smile
Kiss my eyes; or felt the strength spring within
My only son's arms; or sat quiet while
The middle one danced for me, tall and thin.
    All loss is no loss when compared to this:
    To lose your children and their sacred kiss.

9

That you are beautiful let me proclaim.
And that that beauty should be mine to see
Is a blessing which is too great to name.
For, by grace, calling you a friend to me
Is riches far beyond compare. But what
Temptation lurks within our warm bond of
Love? What Satanic traps are set that shut
Around our hearts keeping us from real Love?
Our beating hearts are gripped by such a fear
We tremble 'neath Satan's well devised plan,
Designed to capture that which is by sheer
Beauty lured, adding another fallen man.
    But why should I fear the beauty I see,
    When your beauty is all in all to me.

10

What is this? I can find no peace of mind.
Tormented day and night by my heart's flight
From me. Come back my heart where I can find
What's rightfully mine. Light up this black night
In which my soul is now shrouded. But O'
I feel pleasant hurt at my heart's wand'ring
And though I wrestle with hurt, yet I know
I am beat to submission, wondering
If I will ever be at rest. It is
You who have done this to me: you've taken
My heart into your bosom with a kiss —
My heart, your heart, my own life forsaken.
> Please, lock my heart away in safe keeping
> Or I'll lose my life to mournful weeping.

I I

Where are you most blissful Sleep who bears my
Body beyond this earthly veil where heart
Ache is no more? I cry and I cry,
But you do not hear. Late at night I start
This pining, whining, pleading, yearning for
You to come to me. Are you so callous
That a man in despair you would ignore?
Burdens of the day treat me with malice;
All saints gather together to deplore
Your lack of compassion. But why do I
Blame you, impartial Sleep, when I am sure
That it is lost love that robs me: I die!
    Sleep, O' blissful Sleep, come in spite of me:
    Soothe me with the balm of eternity.

12

Absence, by seldom seeing, is made far
Worse than seeing never. Never seeing
Brings forgetfulness of the only star
Which once shined so bright in my life-being
Once always in its presence, now tortured
By its occasional glimmer, captured
By my ever-seeking eyes. Once nurtured
By its radiant glow, enraptured
By the shedding of Love 'round about me,
Now, my soul is in final darkness lost.
For what was once very dear to now be
Seen every now and then is a high cost.
    If you must go, then be gone forever.
    Seeing seldom is worse than seeing never.

13

The mockingbird sings a joyous song to
The heavens and it echoes deep within
My soul. The melody carries me through
Green valleys of the mind where I begin
To recall fond memories of when Love
Was still young; and to the *now* where my heart
Dwells on you — you being to me songs of
Life. So sing gentle spirit, sing. Depart
Never from my presence; remain until
I am over-full of your song. My soul
Will burst forth in song to its true love still.
Your song is my song, the infinite whole.
    For this I love you all my life long:
    You have inspired in me a joyous song.

14

You are to me as the rain to the grass;
Without you the summer's sun burns me.
As the moon's set in its orbit, alas,
My soul swings around you; and this surely
Is my destiny. Flowers don't grow when
The sun is cloaked by winter's veil; leaves
Fail at December's bitter, chilling wind;
Life's sorrow a most mournful pattern weaves,
Covering my eyes so that I see not
Beyond the dimension of despair in
Which I am now trapped. O' what a sad lot
Are most men who have failed your love to win.
    Flowers grow, and flowers fade; spring's leaves die,
    But your love sustains me through all, I cry!

15

When you are old and gray, and your outward
Beauty is taken away; when Time's hand
Has crossed your face, thus sending you forward
Into Death's shadowy veil, firmly stand
In this knowledge: Beauty's not beauty which
Outward lines define, nor by eye described.
It's the soul's proclivity, the pitch
Of the character to Light, circumscribed
By it, and radiated from within.
When truth is spoken beauty shines brightest;
When false desires are subdued, it is then
That your beauty is indeed the ripest.
    For outward lines do outward beauty show;
    But inner beauty few of us do know.

16

Where've I gone astray that my reins within
Me are consumed by the fire of my
Passions? My soul's aflame with my own sin:
Desiring to live, yet wanting to die.
O' that I might be released from this
Torment: that Melchezedek himself might
Bless me, and bring me peace; or that with his
Mysterious hand he might touch me. Light
Is my soul's eyes seeking from darkness to
Remove this black night into which I've slipped,
Snuffing hell's cold flames, birthing me anew.
I feel as if all's lost, my life short-clipped.
    Counterfeit love has done this unto me:
    Shipwrecked my soul upon life's stormy sea!

17

I did not think it would affect me so:
Seeing you again after so short of
An absence. What I feel I do not know.
I am afraid to call it sacred love.
Love too short a lease has had for a price
Far beyond its worth. What can I say in
Defense of what I feel love has done. Twice
I have fallen. Perhaps to the first sin
I have capitulated — another
Man lost to lust, a shameful waste of spirit.
Fool am I to think I will not smother
My Soul's seeking of Light, losing merit.
    If this temptation is too great for me,
    Hopelessly lost in love I'll always be.

18

I knew that I should not have trusted my
Emotions when first I looked into your
Eyes; that the day'd come when I'd know they'd lie.
For now you have gone off to another,
And I am left only these sad rhymes to
Repeat an often repeated tale of woe.
We most often do what we wish not to;
Hurting where we wished not to hurt. Even so
The damage is done and my poor heart bleeds.
What foolishness we breed who hope to find
Comfort from pain, fulfillment of our needs
When all we have to draw from's our own kind.
    Real Love my heart will ever be seeking,
      'Til this body mine lies with death reeking.

19

The metaphysic that brought us both here
And united our wandering spirits,
Grieves deep at our departing. A lone tear
Bears witness to the loss. Nothing merits
Such sacrifice of emotional joy.
The true name of false sacrifice is waste:
A shameful disgrace by evil deployed.
This estrangement has left such a bad taste
In our mouths where yesterday honey
Was the memory of our kiss; the seal
Of a friendship which made our lives sunny.
So what has been accomplished by this steal:
    It's created a sad me, a sad you;
    I think I shall cry; it's all I can do.

20

How can I suffer such a vile deceit,
When each moment my poor heart breaks in two?
Must I bear it all in my own conceit?
Tormented night and day, desiring to
Be whole again. Flesh and blood were not
Meant to suffer such, they will waste away.
I thought my love pure, but my lust was hot;
I trusted when doubts my trust tried to waylay.
So now, being brought to my knees by You;
Being made to see my error in this:
Forsaking Your lead, and missing my due;
And all for the want of a young bride's kiss.
    Thanks be to You who helps us all to see,
    The failure is not in You, but in me!

21

Truth is precious. No one can disagree.
That Love's all no one's able to debate.
For Truth is Love's argument, its decree;
And Love witnesses for Truth against Hate.
But who among us seeks Truth first and last?
Who is able to discern Love from Lust?
Love testifies for Truth which holds us fast,
And shows us what Love can do. Yet we trust
Wealth and riches above all, forsaking
That which nourishes and protects our lives;
Making us rich in character, taking
Nothing in return — life lost with our sighs.
    All acknowledge Truth and Love being best
        But when brought to life's task, all fail the test.

22

You are unfair in this: my love rejecting.
Seeing that all my hours are spent in
Gathering bouquets from unsuspecting
Gardens; and scheming so that I might win
You from your lofty perch, thus bringing you
Down to the valley where my green love dwells —
Trying, planning, doing all I can do,
Seeking the stars and depths fortunes to tell.
My past faults long ago knifed your bare heart;
The red blood coloring your pride's judgment
Against me, turning you against my part.
This wrong should have caused my begrudgement.
    But how could I ever against you rile,
    When I know that I would myself defile?

23

When you caressed me last evening
My mind refused to believe what my heart
Felt as you were upon my chest leaning.
You were a rose petal to my touch. Are
You true or do I breed phantoms of love,
Weaving patterns from fibers of the air?
What is there to me that one far above
In innocence and purity would dare
To share her bouquet? I am living in
Awe of your look; fear that your touch will send
Me trembling; that my impoverished soul when
It seeks to mingle with yours, will not blend.

> But caress me once again forever,
> And my soul shall depart from you never.

24

The light which shines brightest shines from within;
And the star which guides the soul never sets.
Birds that sing are hushed at the lone heart when
It loves true; pure thoughts the mind never forgets.
The Light of Love is our soul's eyes seeking,
Guiding us back home to those who are our
Mates. Joy in a life is found in speaking
Prayers of love ordained by the Creator.
Nature blossoms forth in colorful song
When two rare spirits ascend to meet;
And when they touch God smiles all the day long;
Sunshine spills from heaven warm hands to greet.
    You shined bright when I gazed into your eyes;
    And my heart replied with such heavy sighs.

25

I am still in a quandary over you;
Not knowing what your fond looks are showing.
Whether or not deception's within you,
Hiding behind beauty's smile that's glowing.
How can I vanquish this flame which within
Me burns if you turn your smile to a frown?
I would be most miserable of men,
If your love gripped my heart and threw me down.
I could then return to my former state:
A shipwrecked sailor out upon the sea
Of life, where I've been searching for my mate.
But what a sad reflection, to be
    Lost. So I shall bide all my time in waiting,
    And place hope in your love not abating.

26

Deep regret, like a heavy burden borne,
Stoops my pained shoulders; and my sunken eye
Lends untruth to my age. My heart is torn
Asunder: I could not live with what I
Most sought: you, my love, your touch and caress.
Cruel Fate said no to me though he brought me
Within your sphere. I am under duress
Of love unrequited. Failing to see
To throw off this weight I must you forget.
But how can I crush the sweet flower of
Remembrance, when to do so disorbits
Me from the solar system of your love?
    Say you love me true and I shall forget,
    You are the cause of my deepest regret.

27

Years ago, when I watched you walk past
My window, I could not tell then what joy
Our souls meeting would bring; and that at last
Love would its sweet secrets to me deploy.
The hands of Time pushed us so far apart
That my mind could not leap the gulf between
Or find the abode of my wayward heart.
For all I saw the truth remained unseen.
But O' Time, you arch deceiver of men,
Your hands followed a circle most divine
Until you brought us together again;
And the *not mine* has now become *mine.*

>O' love, spite your shyness, come to me now;
>And let us take that most sacred vow.

28

The two of you have made the two of me.
Myself fights hard against myself in quest of
Both. One of you on looking's hard to see;
The other possesses the depths of Love.
This quake has split my trembling soul in two.
The fault lies along a dual yearning
Which runs the length of my being. To do
Without the one would cause my mind's burning;
The other's loss would abysmalize me.
So my loves are a wedge that drives me twain;
I am like a giant mahogany
That my two lovers have the heart of slain.
> Now I am forced to the point of choosing;
> Knowing to choose one's to both be losing.

29

My heart can't fight against the thought of you.
I cannot win the battles which are fought
To conquer my soul for the general who
Employs enchanted traps in which I'm caught.
Secret eyes are darts which wound my bear heart;
Your voice is a song which lulls tired troops
To sleep; your smile is a disguise so smart
That I, my own general, before you stoops;
Your hand's a weapon that paralyzes:
I cannot move to my defense at your
Touch. Your gaze is one that hypnotizes
While you slay me at your heart's sacred door.
    If I die, then let my resurrection
    Be service to love by your election.

30

Farewell, a sad farewell to you my friend
In this life where real love is but a ghost.
It's no surprise the two of us must end.
For all things temporal that we love most
Like spring flowers fade, leaving behind sweet
Odors, brief reminders of what has been.
But in dead flowers lies living meat
For a new birth giving us hope to win
At long last the prize we here sought in vain.
So let us not despair in this our loss.
Friendship, though exacting a price of pain,
Paid in remorse of soul is worth the cost.
> Call it no loss when friends from each must part;
> The seed of friendship lives within the heart.

31

When they told me that you had been injured;
When that dreaded news assaulted my ear;
I thought, surely they themselves had perjured,
That no harm could have come within your sphere.
But doubting the truth makes truth no less true;
And on finding that Fate had struck you down
I thought, wicked Fate I will quickly sue
For this black deed by evil-duty bound.
Then I heard your voice across the wires
Roll down a perfect salve upon my ear;
Felt the relief a wounded soul requires,
And thus abated a sorrowful tear.
    Nothing's so sad as the loss of a friend,
    Whose life all meaning to my life does lend.

32

O' how I thought that I would forget you!
That the chalk-board of my mind would erase
The words of love which, once penned, seemed so true;
And that we would never again embrace.
My thoughts deceived me and now you are here
Walking beside me where we first walked
Together: among flowers and sincere
Breezes which blew while we stood and talked
Of a friendship which then we sought to find.
You returned to me when I was the most
Alone. Sleeping clouds which hung in my mind
Vanished before your sight like a startled ghost.
    And now I'm standing in your nascent Light
    Which makes the path before me always bright.

33

Circumstances compounded against me.
No relief is found though sought restlessly.
Your image comes to view, it's all I see.
My mind's applied to you diligently.
When battered I stand against the winds of
Despair which have scarred my time-weathered soul
I fondly recall your noiseless grace, love,
And fold within your dove-like wings. I'm bold
To face the hand that presses the wine press
That spills my blood upon the ground which is
Hallowed by my pain. There, you I undress
In full nakedness and find lasting bliss.

    Weighed down in agony I must lament
    The days and months that are not with you spent.

34

I loved you desperately with all too
Much of me. Now I cling to the thought of
Yesterdays when we walked under blue
Skies which now are full of tears for lost love.
There is no me now. My spirit is lost
With you, somewhere out there where the stars sleep.
Existence is covered with winter's frost.
'Neath the cold hand of my days hear me weep.
What sun will shine and warm my frozen heart?
Where is the ax which serves to break the ice
Of my soul? In the tundra's night I start
To cry for a hurt laid upon me twice.

> Once when you said you loved me no longer;
> And now, when my love for you is stronger.

35

If beauty could be all that she did show;
If flowers were the perfume that they breathe
On the emptiness of all that I know
And all that my eyes think that they see,
Then my life would not seem to seep from my
Dull arteries and down the length of me.
I wouldn't hear the everlasting night cry,
Or feel the chill winter's wind restlessly
Press hard upon the window of my soul.
But beauty is not what beauty shows.
Perfume of flowers hangs in the air, cold.
Nothing that my mind thinks is what it knows.
    And though this truth heavy upon me lies,
    What is life if beauty like a flower dies?

36

The bags under my eyes are permanent
From all of the despair that they have seen.
I now turn my gaze to the firmament,
Away from the earth: wretched, cold, and mean.
Pity me my youth, I am growing old —
My thirty-year frame beginning to bend
From sorrow on sorrow past being told.
Once solid thoughts, are driven by the wind.
O' how can I stay my rapid decline?
Wither has fled the flame which fueled my fire
And sustained my youthful soul's incline?
See it in the first autumn's rain expire.
    I fight daily this feared state to reverse,
    Knowing full well death's worms will me inhearse.

37

Leaving you, I saw a star blaze and die
Standing in the tower where sea meets shore.
I heard rare mixes of music reply
To the yearning of my heart, evermore.
Then, within a wave-crash, time's door
Opened my mind, and stepping through I saw
That for which in the past I had hoped for;
I stood before you in trembling awe.
The door shut! Eyes faded to common sight;
Sea winds shook the tower wherein I stood;
And the black-jeweled blanket covered the night.
My soul strained to remember all it could
    Of the vision impressed upon my mind,
    And the mystic Love I'd sought to find.

38

You knocked at my door and I let you in.
I knocked at your door and you stood there, warm.
I hesitated, afraid of you then;
Like you, I had to get out of the storm.
On entering I saw you were not alone;
And I brought with me shadows of the past.
Once seated, you opposite, the seed sown,
I wondered to myself, would this love last?
I departed and did not return for
Fear that my heart would become lost with you.
This lack of faith shut and then locked the door;
I paced the halls not knowing what to do.
    The door was reopened by providence;
    I entered, and I've been here ever since.

39

You are a rose petal to my hand's touch.
You loved me with a passion gifted and rare;
Sent me a rose and surprised me so much,
My mind scarce believes what my heart does dare.
Solitary that red blossom speaks
Boldly of what I had come to think of
As the blush red glow which graces your cheeks;
And the perfumed scent of absentee love.
My deeper self knows full well of this ploy;
Wisdom and understanding doubting such
A beautiful flower could bring this joy
To a base weed. Then you reached out to clutch
> Me close to your warm breast on which I melt.
> The cradle where all sacred love has dwelt.

40

You called me and I awoke from a dream
Of you. Your voice moved my soul to yearning.
I heard my imprisoned love within scream
For liberty at its vessel's burning;
Burning with your heart-flame, dying for love.
You asked for my aid in something so small.
In giving it, I was blessed from above;
Sharing that moment was my all in all.
Your hair caught the glow from my flaming hearth
And your smile lit the darkness of my soul.
You brought to a sad, sparse room life and mirth,
As if in life this were your only goal.
    You are more than everything to me:
    You are the dearest friend a friend could be.

41

If you only knew how in silent hours
I sit thinking only of you; how my
Heart pines within, dreaming of the flowers
Brought me long ago by you; how your eye
Twinkled as you stole a glance toward me,
As if some lonely star resided there.
If you knew, perhaps my nights would not be
Bare; and you would smile, banishing my care.
If you could see the trail of loneliness
I leave behind upon the seashore sand
As I reflect upon your comeliness,
While the wind cries over the barren land,

>Then maybe you would have pity on me
>With a gentle caress down by the sea.

42

Heaven's stars are sentries which guard the night.
My heart is the guardian of your love,
Against the time when some hideous blight
Shall invade your garden and rob you of
Flowers against which no ill wind should blow.
O' how like a soldier would my heart fight.
My passion would burn; red would be the glow
As I bear my sword hastening troubles flight.
Fear not, my love, at the shadows tending;
Weep not at the apparent loss of love.
Strengthen your faith in the truth I'm lending;
Look steadfastly to the heavens above.
    My heart is a warrior of vigilance,
    Proving in care of love no negligence.

43

I often feel sure, that you must love me;
That your heart, like mine, must sorely lament
A love which seems like it will never be.
That all joys and pleasures it must invent,
From dreams and romantic tales; and must cry
Such lonely tears, the least of which can drown
Two lovers hopelessly lost in a sigh.
But neither of us should lament or frown;
Neither must a single tear shed. For who
Bewails what God has granted as blessed?
Why do we question? No need to be blue.
Our love our life has already confessed:

> Whenever we embrace and part in trust;
> When still, to think of the other's a must.

44

Dearest, I love you. That's all I can say —
Though for fear of your loss I would those words
Take back. A frightened heart is sometimes a
Difficult thing to contain, like some birds
Caged by an innocent admirer's needs.
But how can I hinder my heart's desires
From expressing themselves in heartfelt deeds,
Designed to win that for which it aspires.
Some divine architect made us the same;
Fashioned us so that we would each other
Cherish; that our wild love we'd seek to tame.
For you are Love's sister, I'm Love's brother.
> Take my hand, and complete the divine plan.
> For you are my Woman, and I your Man.

45

"I Love You," is an old and time-worn phrase;
Often used to seduce, transform and gain
Advantage by means of false, empty praise.
Flowers have been the instrument of love
By which many a woman's been beguiled
Of her fairest virtues sent from above.
Like innocence that blesses a child.
If I should happen to say, "I Love You,"
Don't believe me, lest your unguarded heart
Is slain by the very same person who
Sent you beautiful flowers at the start.
    If I say, "I Love You," don't believe me.
    Lest you are caught in love's duplicity.

46

I think of you, my love, far, far too much:
When silence, like a thief, upon me steals.
I find myself remembering your touch,
Or a glance that your sacred love reveals.
I lie upon my pillow at night still,
Quiet, reflecting how you girlishly
Tease me with your tongue, subduing my will
So that my young heart behaves churlishly.
I did not seek you out, or go courting —
Our meeting was serendipitous, and
I found myself my intent aborting;
The house that I had built on shifting sand.
> The truth is, you have become all my thought;
> The meaning of your life is all I've sought.

47

I was no match for you. You conquered me
Despite embattlements erected sound —
Ill-achieved through clandestine strategy.
That peace letter, which your cohorts sent, found
Lying on the pillow within my tent
Told of how you tired of the conflict.
So while I pondered, my heart in a splint
From the last darts you did on me inflict,
You stole round my camp in self-imposed chains.
I, seeing you bound that way, melted down;
And while in my liquid state took great pains
To free you. Freed, you took me for your own.
    In your prison camp, red and warm, I'm bound
    The only place of rest I've ever found.

48

Somewhere, as I for she, my true love waits;
At this moment she thinks of me and writes.
I will read those words ordained by the fates,
Signaled to her by stars on sleepless nights.
Against our union evil has conspired:
A false love, a broken dream, dejection,
All by reason of our haste inspired.
Why I sit in lonely rejection
Of what faith has given me to know,
I cannot tell — unless it's because of
The sharp pains solitude brings. Constant woe
Accompanies my waiting on real love.
    On you I'd rather wait a thousand years
    All through the loneliness, pain and tears!

49

Sometimes, I see your face, how it shines;
As if I gazed a star in the night of
My despair. And O' how my heart pines
For the reality of sacred love.
No thought, morbid or hopeless could displace
The affections I bear for you. Nothing
However tragic could ever erase
The silent words spoken by your smile. Something
Of the mystical has taken place here,
That beguiles me of solitude and rest
With constant thought of your presence so dear,
And anxiety deep within my breast.
    Nothing in nature can with you compare,
    Your beauty is priceless, gifted and rare.

50

Low clouds and fog from the ocean drift in,
Covering the land in a blanket of gray.
The night is dark, still as it's ever been;
I find myself listing, slipping away.
No gull cries, no wind blows; but the fog horn
Moans in the mist as waves crash on the shore.
Feelings, fathoms deep within me are born;
I know them well, they have surfaced before.
The ebb and flow, the heart's beat and after-beat
Are the life force that binds me to the sea.
I step through the veil to find complete
Release in the arms of eternity.
    The littoral washing of the land
      Leaves behind footprints on soulful sand.

51

When I sit in casual wonderment
Of all that my five senses have gathered,
It always seems such an encumberment
To recall that which my mind has tethered.
Things are often other than they appear,
And there is more to a shadow than shows.
As when joy is sometimes shown as a tear;
And what a person thinks he knows
By reason, is by faith shown to be lies.
A person who knows how to truly live
Never really believes that one dies,
But for Truth is prepared his life to give.
    I never knew time did not really exist
    Until I wondered how my watch could subsist.

52

I will sit and I will brood over these words
Until I extract from them the essence
Of you; and return to you that which you deserve,
Always rejoicing within your presence.
A presence I have known only by pen.
O' how your hand is poetry to me;
And O' how my mind it revels within
That lyrical progression of homily.
I have lain awake at night in my bed
Listening to the night bird's melody;
And often of wise men heard it said
That romance in love is Man's folly.
> But in my lonely state I'd rather read,
> Taking the measure of my most quiet need.

53

Your soul is a lovely and timid thing
Whose light-tread I strained to hear approach.
As near it came I heard the angels sing,
And I feared I would receive your reproach.
We poets often peer with prying eyes
Where lowly man is forbidden to see.
We are contracted as earthly spies
To steal back paradise lost and glory
Forsaken for too much love of our minds.
But I am a poor agent of my sphere,
And seeing you have lost the will that binds
Me to my allegiance. One thing is clear:
    On seeing you I've become a counter spy;
    To protect your glory, I'd gladly die!

54

I have seen how the chill hand of winter
Rapes the landscape of the essence of life,
And how fire gone mad leaves untouched no splinter.
I've sung lamentations of human strife;
I've seen how pain can darken young girl's eyes;
And the unmistakable lines of age
Drawn by death's own hand; how vanity cries
As the wind of error turns our last page.
Must the stripes of experience hurt so?
Must my poor young heart become a millstone
Whose weight crushes me beneath the snow?
Is my prison walking this world alone?
    O' great gods, say it is not so; not so;
    Light once again the fire of beauty's glow.

55

The pain that I feel lies too deep for tears;
The kiss of death is upon my forehead.
I have realized my most feared of fears.
All my hope and faith lies within me, dead.
I am so tired of reaching deep within,
I have no strength left to fight the good fight;
I see dimly the prize I'd sought to win;
Darkness has swallowed visionary Light.
When will I have done with these over-sad rhymes
That ring like the death-knell within my ears?
Will these endless melancholy chimes
Turn again to music of friendly spheres?
    My mind's become a sad and lonely place
    With no logic with which to plead its case.

56

Do I doubt that your deeds toward me are true?
That I did not hear your voice across the wires?
I cannot tell if you are the one who
I held last night or if my senses are liars.
If Truth is true, then why is it that I doubt?
Are you Romance's woman sent to beguile,
Telling me with you I can't do without —
The red place in my breast trembling all the while?
O' no, they're the most despicable lies!
The level of my blood's pulse measures my need,
Thrills with the nascent moment of our sighs
While passionately my hungry spirit feeds.
    Doubts may plague me keeping me from my rest,
    But for your love I'll humbly stand this test.

57

Have you ever seen a woman gently
Caressing the strong hands of a man,
And the strength she derives therefrom? Intently
She strokes and lulls; confusion is her plan.
When she has him finely melted down
She bathes within his extracted essence.
Drunk with her power newly found
She dances wildly within his presence.
It isn't long before he begins to
Resent this woman's quest for power,
And sets out to seek a new maid who
He can win again with a flower.
> But there are no maids with flowers to be won
> Who will not leave a strong man quite undone.

58

Can't recall the first time I saw your face,
Or when I first heard the mockingbird sing.
The date, the time and that hallowed place
Are lost within the cares that suffering brings.
O' how I have suffered since first we met.
Your rose-soft touch wounded me mortally,
Placing in my mind wonder I can't forget.
You are the cause of all my poetry!
By social decree I can no longer
Feel your eyes; melt at your touch; kiss your lips.
A single glance from you would make me stronger
Though my reasoned mind daily from me slips.
    For a single glance I would forfeit all;
    And like a sun's planet ever towards you fall.

59

I was touched by your tears the night you cried:
Your soft, brown eyes glistened behind the rain.
For too much of humanity has died,
And all men of principle have been slain.
Soulful wellsprings can't wash bloody streets clean;
Hearts that burn with hate can't bring back the dead.
The peace we seek to win must not be mean,
But must be won by sacrifice that's bled
From the common artery of mankind.
Though your silent weeping awakened me
To your deep sense of care, I cannot find
A reason to share in your misery.
    But hang your pride on the tree, let it die,
    And mankind will have no reason to cry.

60

Sin of self-doubt is all my destruction
Laying to waste the very soul of me.
I have failed to heed Divine Instruction;
Forsaking the truth for pain and misery.
Believing a lie makes the lie seem
Like Truth, and makes Truth seem like a liar.
But Truth from the grave more loudly will scream
'Til all of your being's ablaze with fire.
All this the world knows yet none knows how
To remove all doubt and live once again.
All seem to prefer the ear of the sow
And feel not alive 'less reminded by pain.
    Learn this one lesson, and learn it well:
    The sin of self-doubt leads all men to hell.

61

Primeval whisperings, buzzing of bees;
Wind whispered mysteries down the canyon call;
A frightened quail covey for cover flees;
Golden leaves begin their eternal fall.
Birds are singing territorial songs,
Somewhere far, far above a raptor cries.
For a distant time this canyon longs.
On still, moonlit nights you can hear its sighs.
People were here once, much like me and you.
Their lamentations are heard in the wind.
When you stop to drink of this ancient brew,
Made of earth, sky, plants and creatures of rare blend;
    A communion of the soul's taken place
    With the ETERNAL MASTER of Time and Space.

62

A birthday wish from me to you is all
That I can give. I do not have flowers,
Nor diamonds; nor the words with which to call
You my blessed, my own. My spirit cowers
Beneath the weight of human wantonness.
I sorely lament my poetic dearth.
Think! How the world would feel my loneliness
If it did not possess one of your worth,
Born a flower on a late summer day.
The air would know that it had been robbed of
A rare bouquet. So, what can I say?
But that when you were born, so too was love.
    Your birth is the star that I wish upon
    For Love that's shed in the infinite dawn.

63

The last time we embraced, was the last time:
A moment of singular affection.
What a travesty is this silly rhyme
Which attempts to honor that recollection.
We stand two peripatetic souls
Among such a mass of humanity.
As we within our arms the other holds
Onlookers think we're filled with insanity.
But once securely locked within the arms
Of the other the world dissolves away,
And life, which gives so many false alarms,
Is stilled like the benediction of day.
    There is a dimension where true lovers dwell.
    Those who find it can never another tell.

64

Our hearts are made to be given away,
Not our souls. You cannot take that which
Cannot be possessed. And for me to say
That I give you my all would be to pitch
That which is self down into the abyss.
You may tempt the red place in my breast
From me with the sweetness of your kiss
And wear it upon your bosom as a crest;
But the very compass of my being
Which points home to the genesis of life,
And is the fountain-light of all my seeing,
Cannot be the charge of the dearest wife.
    My soul is my most sacred possession;
    My heart to you is my only concession.

65

When the rose upon the vine is grown old
Unfolded from bud to flower full,
What can I say of love that's grown cold
And a mind by much care rendered dull?
The seasons roll onward and the spring
Returns with winds passionately full of
Yesterday's bouquet; I am wont to bring
Myself to echo her whispers of love.
Unlike the spring which returns every year,
When the flower of my love has decayed
I am left standing in singular fear.
There is nothing to do but be dismayed.
    My love, though lovely, is dead and gone
    And though spring returns I'm left here, alone.

66

Nevertheless this fancied song of mine
Can sing no more. For you have taken leave
Of your life. In a cosmic sense that's fine.
But I'm carnal; I'll do nothing but grieve.
The music I played upon the bare page
Is with you now, cold-sepulchered-away;
Awaiting renaissance in another age,
The shedding of Light on that nascent day.
I could sing lamentations of my woe,
Or make disconsonant sounds on my lyre;
But what would be the point to behave so?
No human plight, however grave, is that dire.
    My heart is heavy and there is no rhyme
        That can heal my wounds like the hands of time.

67

How will I write of you when you are gone,
For you are all my music? In your voice
Is my most blessed rhyme. To me you've shown
The harmony that's all the critics' choice.
I'm convinced from you the birds stole their song;
That the music of the spheres is your sigh.
To still those lips was a grievous wrong
When other melody does you belie.
I have but memories now that you are dead
To serve as the score for life's symphony.
By your restless ghost through movements I'm led
Creating a mournful cacophony.
    And if mournful sounds are all I'm to know
    Then being from you woe seems not woe.

68

I walked along the path you once walked;
I sat where you must have sat. I thought,
As I wandered along, of how we talked
And dreamed of the plans that our hearts had wrought.
When the evening chilled and a lonely breeze
Swept past my waiting ear, remembrance filled
Me like the ocean winds fill the trees.
For a light-moment my heart was stilled.
All was new: you hadn't gone away from me;
The white caps tossed their heads merrily
Above the emerald deep. I could see
You rising from the mystic depths of the sea;
    And the moon rising behind you giving birth
    To the night-jewel that crowns all of the earth.

69

With gentle coaxing down endless ages
You began your sculptor's chore; and still
Your tireless progression turns new pages
Of the hallowed book of stone. Working 'til
You had achieved some measure of art,
You did not stop; rather, continued to
Strive with your challenge with courageous heart.
When your art had turned to masterpiece you
Lay down within its bosom, but could not sleep
For awe at your own creation. To hew
Out of stone, canyons which are meant to keep
The infinite progeny of the dew,
    Is a sacred task of obligation
    Of which you are the only oblation.

70

Will time give back to me these empty hours?
Your Presence is all there is to my life.
Your pulse is the force which drives the flower
From green age to infinity. The strife
Between Time and Eternity is naught,
Because in you there is only the *now*.
Of sufferings I need not take any thought
Once I have taken the most sacred vow:
To live within your encompassing scope
(Which I must do if I am to live at all).
Time will not cheat me of my cherished hope
If in my life you your Presence install.
    I return quickly to my lover's side
    Where Time and Eternity co-abide.

71

Summer cannot prevent the full lease
Of winter's stay, though it lingers long
Into the fall. Aged wine cannot ease
The advent of trouble no matter how strong.
Things rush to their appointed conclusion;
You cannot escape the hands of Fate;
All are within predestined inclusion.
When the storm clouds have gathered it's too late
To build an ark. When the rains begin
And the creek rises to the level of
Your transgressions, prayers for remissions of sin
Will fail for want of brotherly love.
    With all of the things we profess to know,
    Why can't we see that we reap what we sow?

72

We cut down the trees to make way for fields:
You can hear the axes ringing, ringing.
Then, silence, while the earth its riches yields;
No more the sound of the wood thrush singing.
We cut highways through our golden grain;
Built houses and factories, steams boats and towns.
Some called it progress, and others insane;
The latter despaired and wore ugly frowns.
Then Progress stepped forward in Death's proud hour,
Beginning his spurious reign:
"If things turn out bad I have the power
To blow things up and start over again."
    The lone wilderness trembles in its stead
    Every time a jet roars overhead.

73

Jurisimprudence has shackled Reason
By black-robed back-city commonsenselessness
Committing the heinous crime of treason
Through misguided legislativemess —
Commonly called government. And who is
It that suffers most from pseudo justice?
The least able to backward reason. This
Taken advantage of populace,
The unborn, unknown spirit, could not
Find the promised land of milk and honey,
Home of the brave, so-called melting pot
'Cause milk and honey costs too much money.
    Justice slain stirs beneath the heavy sod
    And racks painfully the conscience of God.

74

Vision in seeing is much more than sight;
Hate is not only the absence of love;
Darkness is not just the absence of light;
The dove's not spirit but spirit the dove.
Form is not substance and substance not form;
Together they create more than they show.
Stay from creating a standard or norm
Unless you want to know less than you know.
Beware of plans that are laid with such care
They trap the layer in the trap that was laid.
Being where you've been doesn't mean you're there
Paying the piper doesn't mean the debt's paid.
    Open your eyes and you will surely see
    Being's much more than you thought it could be.